For Innes, with all my love.

And to Gill and her Great Auntie Betty.

First published in 2020.

Printed in the United States of America

ISBN 978-1-7348792-0-9

www.vhairijanemoir.com

Book design and illustrations by Veronika Gonchar

Great Auntie Betty
and
The Serengeti

Vhairi Jane Moir

Illustrated by Veronika Gonchar

It was not past
seven-thirty,
on a Sunday morning,
when Great Auntie Betty arrived from the Serengeti.

Mum's and Dad's face said it all,

having not received
a cautionary call.

"My dearest darlings," she trilled.
"It's me!
I am back from my travels from overseas, you see.

I jumped in a taxi and I hopped on a train.
I sailed by boat and I flew by plane."

Great Auntie Betty then wiped her black boots and trundled through, dragging a giant brown trunk stamped **EXPORTS FOR THE ZOO.**

"The wilderness of Africa," the old lady declared, "is the most magnificent thing. Oh, what a stupendous delight it is — where the animal is truly king."

EXPORTS FOR THE ZOO

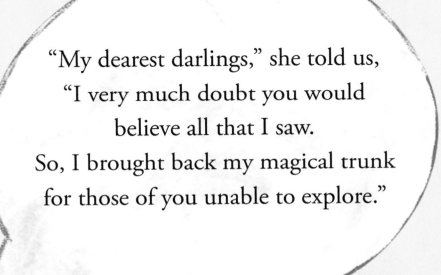

"My dearest darlings," she told us,
"I very much doubt you would
believe all that I saw.
So, I brought back my magical trunk
for those of you unable to explore."

And from that trunk she pulled **1** fierce lion that gave a wild **ROAR**.

It leapt over our heads and charged towards the living room door.

After that came **2** giraffes with long tongues and necks, and bodies covered with their unique print effect.

3 stomping elephants were next, can you believe?

4 black and white zebras followed,

before **5** galloping wildebeests.

Incredible, we thought, what else can be inside?

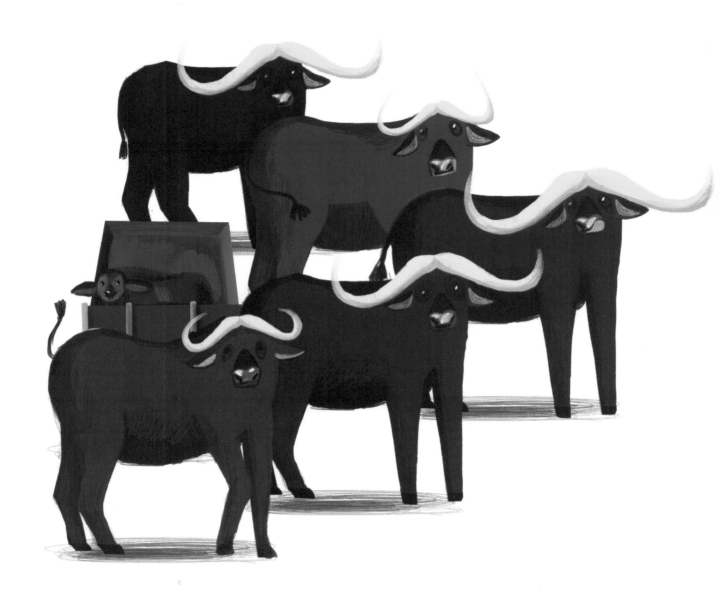

And a gang of **6** buffalo emerged side by side.

Indeed, Great Auntie Betty wasn't done yet,

7 spotted leopards came forth,
and we wondered what would be next?

Out popped **8** mongooses,
and then **9** cobra snakes.
The living room was now jam-packed with animals,
make no mistake.

Last of all was the black rhino –
the most elusive beast.

10 of those with two horns each,
concluded this wonderful, wildlife feast.

Just as Mum and Dad turned very pale, about to faint,

Great Auntie Betty began to holler without a shred of constraint.

Giving her most ferocious call,
animal after animal,
thundered past our sofa; big and small.

Back to that old brown trunk,
went **1** lion and **2** giraffes.
Back went the **3** stomping elephants,
the **4** black and white zebra,
and **5** galloping wildebeests – two of them calves.

Back went the **6** buffalo,
the **7** spotted leopards,
the **8** mongooses and the **9** cobra snakes.
And back went the **10** black rhinos, not one of them late.

Wrestling the jumping lid with an impatient 'tut',
Great Auntie Betty heaved her giant trunk shut.

"Right," she announced, "I'm off to the Arctic.
Yes, dearest darlings, I'm popping over there.

I shall see you all again in twelve months,
in the company of a musk ox,
or perhaps a polar bear."

And off Great Auntie Betty went then,
towing her magical brown trunk behind.

For she favoured the animal kingdom –
far more than humankind.